LET'S·READ·AND·FIND·OUT·SCIENCE®

SWITCH ON, SWITCH OFF

by Melvin Berger

Illustrated by Carolyn Croll

HarperCollinsPublishers

The *Let's-Read-and-Find-Out Science* book series was originated by Dr. Franklyn M. Branley, Astronomer Emeritus and former Chairman of the American Museum–Hayden Planetarium, and was formerly co-edited by him and Dr. Roma Gans, Professor Emeritus of Childhood Education, Teachers College, Columbia University. Text and illustrations for each of the books in the series are checked for accuracy by an expert in the relevant field. For more information about Let's-Read-and-Find-Out Science books, write to HarperCollins Children's Books, 1350 Avenue of the Americas, New York, NY 10019, or visit our website at www.letsreadandfindout.com.

HarperCollins®, ®, and Let's Read-and-Find-Out Science® are trademarks of HarperCollins Publishers Inc.

SWITCH ON, SWITCH OFF

Text copyright © 1989 by Melvin Berger
Illustrations copyright © 1989 by Carolyn Croll

Library of Congress Cataloging-in-Publication Data
Berger, Melvin.
  Switch on, switch off / by Melvin Berger ; illustrated by Carolyn Croll.
    p.   cm. — (Let's read-and-find-out science book)
  Summary: Explains how electricity is produced and transmitted, how to create electricity using wire and a magnet, how generators supply electricity for cities, and how electricity works in homes.
  ISBN 0-690-04784-3. — ISBN 0-690-04786-X (lib. bdg.). — ISBN 0-06-445097-X (pbk.)
  1. Electricity—Juvenile literature.   [1. Electricity.]   I. Croll, Carolyn, ill.   II. Title.   III. Series.
QC527.2.B47   1989   88-17638
537—dc19   CIP
                                                                                                                                    AC

SWITCH OFF

SWITCH ON,

It's time to go to sleep. You go to your bedroom. The room is dark. You flip up the switch on the wall. The light goes on.

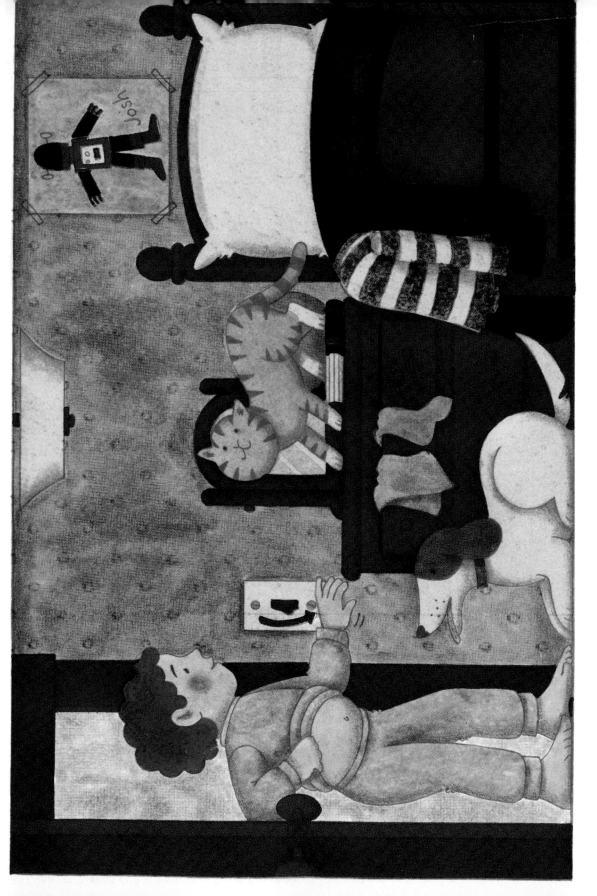

You get into your pajamas. Just before you jump into bed, you flip down the switch. The light goes off.

Flip up—the light goes on. Flip down—the light goes off. It seems like magic. But it's not magic at all. It's electricity!

7

Electricity is a form of energy. Energy is anything that does work.

You have lots of energy. Your energy lets you walk, run, throw a ball, ride a bike—and sometimes even clean your room!

Electrical energy also does work. It lights your house. It brings you sound from your radio. If you have an electric stove, it cooks your food. If you have an air conditioner, it keeps you cool.

Your energy comes from the food you eat. But electrical energy has to be made.

You can make electricity by yourself. You'll need a piece of electrical wire about two yards long. Ask an adult to help strip the insulation off the ends of the wire. You'll also need a bar magnet and a compass. The compass will show whether or not you are making electricity.

1. Wrap one end of the wire around your hand about ten times, to make a coil. 2. Slide the coil off your hand. 3. Now wrap the other end of the wire around the compass about five times. Leave the wire there. 4. Then twist the two metal ends of the wire together to make one big loop.

5. Slide the magnet quickly back and forth inside the coil. This makes electricity flow in the wire. Look at the compass as you do this. Do you see the needle move? The moving needle tells you that electricity is flowing.

5.

But how does electricity flow through a wire? The wire is made up of billions of tiny bits, or particles. They are called atoms. Each atom is much too small to be seen. But each atom has even smaller particles. Some of these move in paths around the atom's center. They are the electrons.

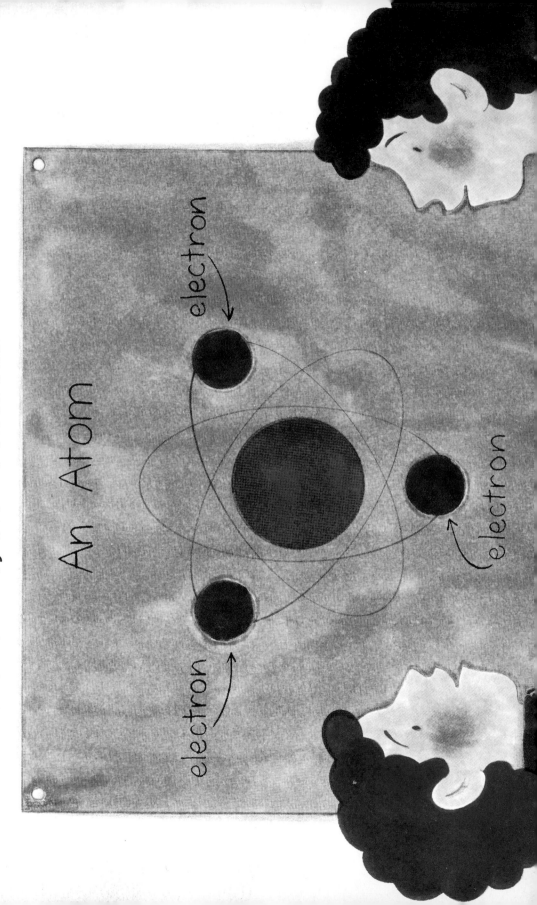

An Atom

electron

electron

electron

Moving the magnet near the wire makes the electrons move out of their paths. They speed from atom to atom. The speeding electrons are what we call electricity.

The opposite works, too. Moving a coil of wire near a magnet also makes electricity flow.

15

Any machine that makes electricity is called a generator. Your little generator made a tiny bit of electricity. But it takes very big generators to supply electricity for a whole city.

GENERATOR

The magnet spins around inside the coils.

These generators have huge coils and giant magnets.
Most generators spin a magnet inside the coils. Others
spin coils between two magnets.

coils

magnet

coils

spinning
magnet

The muscles in your arms supplied the power for your little generator. But big generators need much more power to spin their coils or magnets. This power can come from—

wind....

flowing water....

steam....

burning fuel

As the coils or magnets spin, electricity flows in the coils. The big wire coils are connected to other wires.

spinning magnet

coils

electricity

These wires are strung along the tops of tall poles. The electricity travels through the wires for many miles. Shorter wires branch off from the long wires. They bring electricity to the homes, schools, stores, and other places that need it. One of these wires goes to your house.

wire to house

wire to house

If you live in the country or in a small town, you can probably see the wire that brings the electricity into your house. If you live in a big city, you may not see the wire because it is under the ground.

21

Each wire is really made up of two separate wires. One brings the electricity from the generator into your house. The other takes the electricity back to the generator.

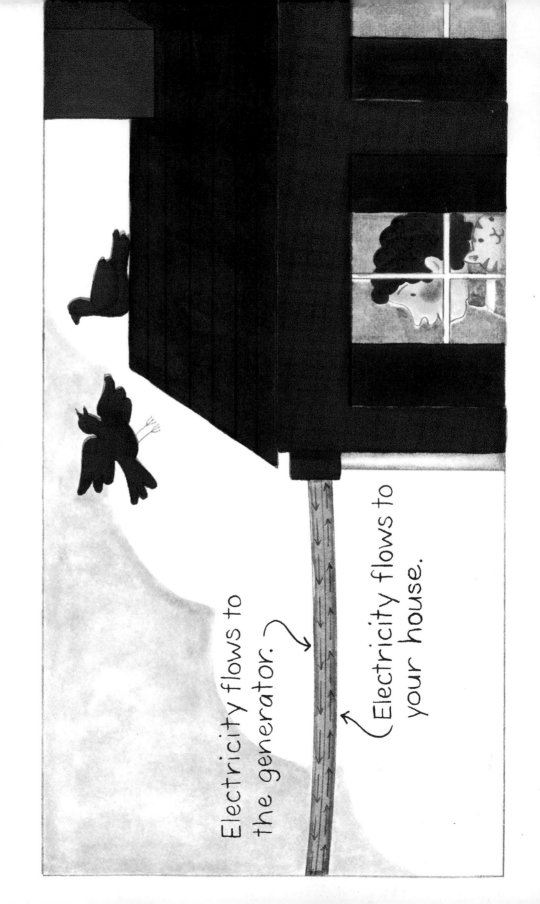

Electricity flows to the generator.

(Electricity flows to your house.

When you made your little generator, you tied the ends of the wire together. That made a loop, or circuit. Electricity always travels in a circuit. It only flows if it can get back to its starting point. If there is a break in the circuit, the electricity does not flow at all.

electricity →

A CIRCUIT

break

The circuit that comes into your house splits into many other circuits. It is like many small roads coming off a big highway. All the circuits in your house have breaks in them. The breaks let you turn the electricity on and off. That's what the switch is for!

The in and out wires of one circuit meet at the light switch in your room. When the switch is down, the break in the wire is open. No electricity can flow. The light is off.

Flip up the switch. The break is closed. Now the electricity can travel through the wire to the bulb on the ceiling. The light goes on.

light on

break closed

switch up

light off

break open

switch down

Inside the bulb, there is a very thin wire. The electricity must squeeze through this wire. When it does, the wire heats up. The wire quickly becomes white-hot. The glow of the white-hot wire in the bulb lights your bedroom.

From the bulb, the electricity zips back to the switch. And from there it returns to the generator.

thin wire

plug

prongs

outlet

Maybe you have a lamp instead of a ceiling light. The lamp has a plug at the end of its wire. The plug has two metal prongs. Electricity can flow through the prongs just as it does through wires.

You fit the plug into an electrical outlet in the wall.

The two wires of the house circuit are connected to the two holes of the outlet. When you put the plug in the outlet, the electricity can flow through the outlet, the plug, and the wire, and into the lamp.

The lamp has a switch. When you turn the lamp switch on, the electricity flows through the bulb and back out through the house circuit.

The next time you get ready for bed, stop and think. "Switch on" means you closed the circuit. The electricity flows.

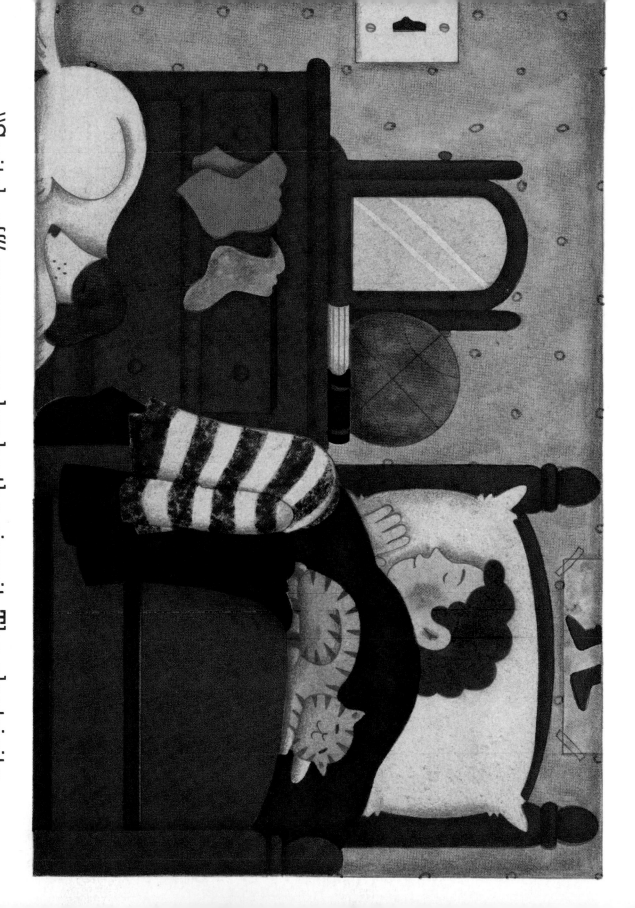

"Switch off" means you broke the circuit. The electricity cannot flow. Then it is dark and time to sleep. Good night. Pleasant dreams.

FIND OUT MORE ABOUT ELECTRICITY

Make Your Own Electricity!

You will need:

a raw potato

a length of copper wire

an iron nail

a piece of paper

1. Insert the copper wire and the nail into the potato, about two inches apart.

2. Hold the piece of paper so that it hangs between the two metals. After a minute, the paper should be attracted to the negatively charged nail and start to move toward it.

The chemicals in the juice of the potato react with the metals and produce an electric current that causes the paper to move.